The Magic Harp

Declan Carville

Illustrated by
Melvin Carroll

For Mum and Dad
D.C.

For Niamh, Aoife and Keelan
M.C.

Discovery Publications
Ireland

Middlemass, from the outside, was not unlike most other country towns.

The Magic Harp

Yet people came from everywhere, just to visit.
Middlemass was famous.

Granny Teasie lived over the grocer's shop and for as long as she could remember the music had always been there. A wonderful sound. Most relaxing. That it was the sound of a harp was undeniable but from where it came exactly - or who was playing it - no one had ever been able to find out.

"Perhaps the fairies have settled on Foley's Hill," said Mrs Ryan in the bakery. "I always knew they'd come back."

Everyone had their own theory, though the real truth was nobody was any the wiser. A newspaper in the city promised a big reward and visitors from America had even talked about making a movie. But that was years ago. Today the people of Middlemass had grown tired of trying to solve the mystery on their own doorstep. The sound of the harp was always there and now they were content to sit back and enjoy it. It had become a part of their lives.

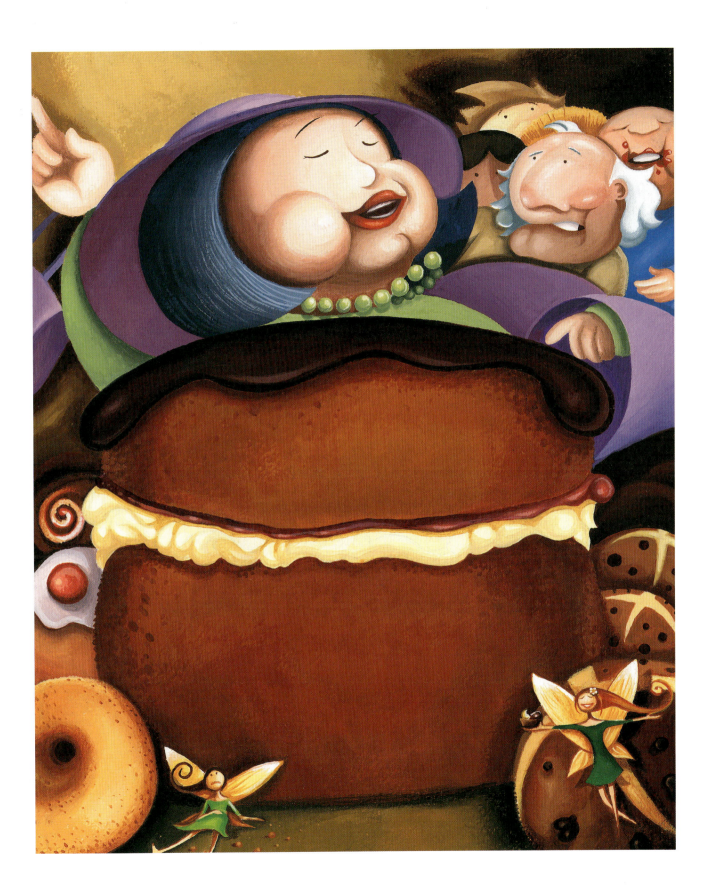

Fergal O'Connor lived in Church Street, at the top of the town next door to the Florist. School may have just finished for the week but as the young boy walked up Main Street he looked far from happy. Miss O'Neill had given them a homework for the weekend and Fergal and the rest of his class were not amused at all.

Homework on a Friday and, to make matters worse, it had to be a story. '*A Trip to Somewhere Exciting.*' What was he going to write about? 'I've never been to anywhere exciting,' Fergal groaned to himself.

When he reached the house Fergal went straight to the kitchen and poured himself a glass of juice from the fridge. He tried to think of a potential storyline. 'The seaside? Last year's holiday to Spain? A visit to Uncle Michael's? Bah! It has all been done before!' he frowned. He began to search in one of the cupboards for the biscuit tin but was interrupted by a knock on the window. It was Maureen, from the shop next door.

"For your mother, Fergal," she said, extending both arms, overflowing with flowers. "And tell her I don't want any money for them. They were left over from a big order."

"I'll tell her," said Fergal. "Thank you Maureen."

The smell of the flowers filled the kitchen - reds, yellows and greens, with enough left over for every room in the house. Fergal's Mum would be pleased. She loved to have plants and flowers all over the place and Maureen was forever ordering too many. 'I suppose I could always write a story about the forest,' Fergal thought to himself, setting the flowers on the table. 'It would be different, and we have had some great adventures there.' He paused to take in the scent of the foliage. 'If I gathered some leaves and twigs and stuck them in my homework book,' he continued, a smile breaking on his face, 'Miss O'Neill would be really pleased...'

What a transformation! Now Fergal couldn't wait to get started. He set down his glass of juice and began to lay the table for dinner later that day with his Mum and two younger sisters. 'If I get this done now,' he whispered to himself, 'it means I can begin right away...'

Fergal knew the forest well. They loved to play among the trees - it was such fun compared to the back garden. Collecting the leaves for his story, however, was proving more difficult than he had thought. His back was starting to ache and he had just about made up his mind that he had done enough when a bright light ahead interrupted his concentration. Fergal looked up towards the sky. He wondered if a spaceship was about to land, but all he could see was the gentle swaying of the branches above his head. He walked a little further until at last he came to a clearing.

Fergal couldn't believe what he saw.

"Lady with the harp," he stammered,
afraid to go any further. There had been
so much talk in town, he didn't know
what to expect, or what to do next.
    "That's right," she replied in a gentle voice,
barely raising her eyes to look in his direction.
    "My name's Fergal," he whispered.
    "Yes," said the lady, "I know."

All around him Fergal could hear the wind passing through the old oak and chestnut trees, but it was the sound of the harp that filled the forest air.

"I thought you were a spaceship..." he began to mumble, overwhelmed by his new discovery. Fergal noticed that the lady had long red hair and wore a dress that covered much of the ground.

"Do you like my music?" she asked, smiling in his direction.

"I do," replied Fergal. "Everyone does. You're famous - all over the country."

"I'm pleased," said the lady as she continued to play.

Fergal hesitated a moment. "What's your name?" he asked, moving a little closer. But the lady made no reply. Her gaze rarely strayed from the strings of the harp and only for the graceful movement of her hands through the air, she hardly stirred at all.

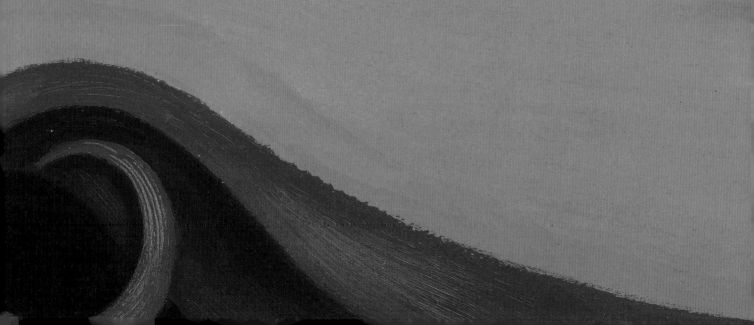

"I was wondering," she said at last, "if you could keep a secret?"

"I can," replied Fergal, without a moments hesitation.

"Then come back tomorrow," she said, "but be sure to tell no one what you have seen. Come in the afternoon, and I'll grant you a wish."

"I will," he said. "To this same place?" But the lady had lowered her head and appeared as distant as ever.

Standing alone under the shade of the old chestnut tree Fergal could feel the butterflies in his tummy. He didn't want to go, but he knew he ought to be heading home soon. 'No need for these now,' he thought to himself, staring at the leaves in his hands. It was strange to think that only a short while ago he had been so careful to select the best he could find. But his plans had changed. Already Fergal was thinking of a new story for his homework book.

Saturday morning. Fergal loved Saturday mornings. In fact, it was his favourite time of the week.

This particular Saturday, however, was more special than ever before. All night long he lay awake listening to the sound of the harp. 'But what if it was all a dream,' he thought to himself. 'What if she is from outer space...?' Fergal couldn't stop wondering if the lady would still be there. Chores all done, he waved goodbye and set off in the direction of the forest.

"Have fun!" shouted his Mum as she closed the backdoor behind him.

At last Fergal reached the clearing in the middle of the forest. He was sure it was the same place he had been the day before.

"Fergal, over here!" came a voice.

Fergal looked behind him. And there she was. The lady with the harp.

"I knew you would come back!" she said. "I just knew it."

"I didn't tell anyone," said Fergal.

"Our secret," smiled the lady.

Fergal felt so pleased with himself. He suddenly remembered the time he won a gold star in school during 'Show and Tell', when he had gone to the front of his class and told everyone about the boomerang Uncle Kevin had sent him from Australia. And then there was the time he made his Mum

breakfast in bed on her birthday. But this was different. From among all the people in town and everyone who had come to hear the music for themselves, he was the only one who knew the truth. It was their special secret.

"And what about your wish?" asked the lady. "Have you any ideas?"

"I do," replied Fergal, taking a deep breath.

"And...?" she said.

"Can I go to the moon?" he asked.

"The moon?" she repeated. "Have you been before?"

"Never," replied Fergal.

"I've heard it's terribly cold. Have you got a hat with you?" Fergal shook his head. It was nearly June, he thought to himself. He hadn't worn a hat in months.

"Hmme..." she replied. "Then we'll have to see what we can do."

The lady stood up from her seat at the side of the harp and called him forward.

"This way Fergal," she said, "just keep following the path."

Fergal thought he was going to explode with excitement. All around him the forest swayed to the most heavenly sound as the lady held the strings apart and invited him to step through to the other side.

"Careful!" she smiled, moving out of his way. "Here - take hold of
my hand."

Fergal could feel himself beginning to shake all over. As he lowered his
head he was just about to ask if he could be back in time for dinner when
he suddenly became lost for words. From behind the mass of red hair
Fergal had caught sight of a pair of wings.

The moon was cold. Cold and quiet. No plants or trees.
No birds or animals. Nothing at all.

Fergal tried running over the moon's surface, but it was very difficult to make up any speed. Everything was in slow motion. He took another look around him. The ground was covered in sand, but not like the golden sand at the seaside. On the moon it looked grey. He tried running up and down again. He even performed a few handstands. Darragh Murphy, his best friend at school, always tried to push him over when he managed a handstand. They pushed each other. But there was no one else here to join in. Fergal began to miss his Mum and his sisters and all his friends at home. Saturday was his favourite day of the week and he was going to miss it all if he didn't get back soon... 'If I could just build up enough speed,' he thought to himself. He gazed around and was about to take a giant leap into the darkness when...

Bump!!!

.... he landed on a clump of ferns
on the forest floor. The lady was
standing waiting nearby.

"Ohhh!" she said, quite surprised. "I was beginning to wonder where you had got to. Did you have a good time, Fergal?"

"I did. Thank you," he replied, dusting himself down.

"You have been gone for quite a while," she said. "Was it a good adventure?"

"Oh yes," replied Fergal, not wanting to appear ungrateful. "But I was thinking - I might wish for something different next time. That's if I can come back and see you again?" he asked, shaking the last of the leaves from his sweater.

"Come any time," she said. "I'm always here."

Once again Fergal found himself standing in the shade of the huge chestnut tree. Everything had returned to just how it was before. Over his head leafy branches swayed in the gentle breeze, while the fading rays of the afternoon sunlight bathed all around in a warm summer glow.

Fergal watched as the lady took her seat at the side of the harp, her hands beginning to dance over the strings of the magical instrument. 'Just a few minutes more and then I'll go,' he thought to himself. But the lady never did raise her head to look back.

The town clock in Middlemass was striking six as Fergal reached the top of Main Street. He had been gone the whole afternoon. Shops were closing their doors after another busy day and in the distance he could see his Mum chatting to Granny Teasie outside the grocer's window.

"Mummmmmm!!!" he shouted, as he ran up to meet her, burying his head in her side.

"My word!!!" said Granny Teasie. "Somebody's pleased to see you!"

"Careful Fergal," said his Mum, "or you'll knock me over!"

Fergal could tell right away that his Mum had been busy. Shopping bags overflowing with the weekly groceries lay scattered all around.

"Had a nice time then?" asked his Mum.

"Oh yes," he replied, taking a peek to see what she had bought.

"And I suppose you're ready for your dinner now?" she smiled. "I guess it's time we were heading back. Bye Teasie."

Fergal rushed forward to give his Granny a hug.

"A strong boy like you Fergal," said Granny Teasie, "man of the house now, I'm sure you're going to help your Mammy carry the shopping home?"

Fergal turned to gather a few of the bags together. "I can carry them all if you like!" he smiled.

"My word!" exclaimed the old lady. "Just look at the state of those hands! What have you been up to child?"

Fergal held out his arms for closer examination. They were covered in sand!

"Never mind, love," smiled his Mum. "You can have your bath before dinner tonight. See you tomorrow Teasie."

"Make sure he eats his greens, Moira," shouted Granny Teasie, leaning on her stick, "or he'll never grow up big and strong!"

"Oh, he always eats his greens Teasie," she replied. "Now you get back inside and put your feet up."

As another summer evening was about to descend on the little town of Middlemass, mother and son turned to face the short walk home, arms laden with groceries.

"Shopping all over for another week," she sighed as they passed the Post Office. "I think I'll have a relaxing bath myself tonight, Fergal. I feel so tired."

Fergal's Mum loved to listen to the sound of the harp, and as they walked together along the deserted pavement, she began to sing to the gentle rhythm of the music.

"I wish every day could be like Saturday, Mum," said Fergal, rearranging the heavy bags in his hands.

"Wouldn't that be good..." she smiled, "but today is Saturday, and I was thinking - we could have a surprise tonight..."

"What surprise?" shouted Fergal. "Tell me Mum, please!!!"

"Only if you can keep a secret..." she said, looking straight ahead. "What do you think... could you?"

"Yes Mum!" exclaimed Fergal. "Of course I can keep a secret!"

"Well..." she continued, the excitement rising in her own voice, "I was going to cook chips tonight, as a special treat. But you're not to tell the others or it will just spoil everything."

"Cool!" shouted Fergal. "We haven't had chips in ages! Can we have them watching our programmes on TV?"

"We'll see," she said. "And if you're good - all of you, really, really good - then there might be some ice cream for afters."

First published in Ireland by Discovery Publications,

Brookfield Business Centre, 333 Crumlin Road, Belfast BT14 7EA

Tel; 028 9049 2410 • e-mail; declan.carville@ntlworld.com

Text © 2004 Declan Carville • Illustrations © 2004 Melvin Carroll

A CIP catalogue reference of this book is available from the British Library

Designed by Melvin Carroll.

Printed in Belgium by Proost.

ISBN 0-9538222-7-3

1 2 3 4 5 6 7 8 9 10